Dora's Big Dig

by Alison Inches
illustrated by Robert Roper

Simon Spotlight/Nick Jr.

New York   London   Toronto   Sydney

Based on the TV series *Dora the Explorer*® as seen on Nick Jr.®

SIMON SPOTLIGHT
An imprint of Simon & Schuster Children's Publishing Division
1230 Avenue of the Americas, New York, New York 10020
© 2006 Viacom International Inc. All rights reserved.
NICK JR., *Dora the Explorer*, and all related titles, logos, and characters are
registered trademarks of Viacom International Inc.
All rights reserved, including the right of reproduction in whole or in part in any form.
SIMON SPOTLIGHT and colophon are registered trademarks of Simon & Schuster, Inc.
Manufactured in the United States of America
2 4 6 8 10 9 7 5 3
ISBN-13: 978-1-4169-0806-7
ISBN-10: 1-4169-0806-4

¡Hola! I'm Dora, and today I'm digging in the garden.
Dig! Dig! Dig!

Wow! I uncovered a turquoise stone. Ooooh, maybe this is an ancient treasure!

I should take this stone to my *mami*. My *mami* is an
archeologist. That means she digs for ancient treasure!
She'll know what to do with an ancient treasure.

First I need to pick up my friend Boots.

Look, Boots! The stone has a jaguar's face carved into it, and the jaguar is wearing a crown.

Boots and I are going to need *your* help to get to the pyramid to see my *mami*. Who do we ask for help when we don't know which way to go? Yeah, the Map! Say "Map!"

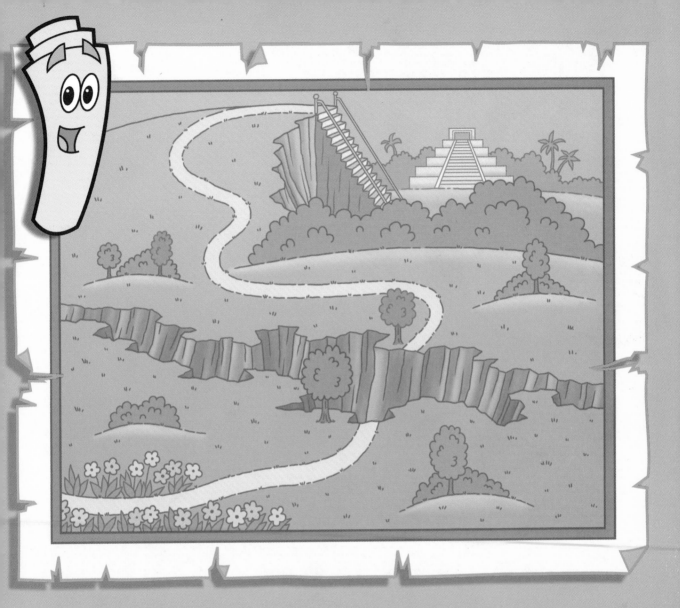

Map says that we have to go across Emerald Canyon. Then we have to climb down the Steep Steps, and that's how we'll get to my *mami*.

¡Vámonos! Let's go!

Do you see Emerald Canyon? There it is! But it's so deep!
How are we going to get across? Do you see something we
can use to zip over the canyon?
Yeah! We can use the zip cord!

Wheeeee!

We made it over Emerald Canyon!

Uh-oh! Do you see Swiper? I think that sneaky fox wants to swipe our turquoise stone. We have to stop him. Quick! Say "Swiper, no swiping!"

Thanks for helping us stop Swiper. Where do we go next?
That's right—the Steep Steps!

Do you see the Steep Steps? There they are!

Wow, these steps are really steep! Let's hold on to the rail.

We have to climb down ten steps. Will you help us count? ¡Uno, dos, tres, cuatro, cinco, seis, siete, ocho, nueve, diez!

We made it down the Steep Steps! Good counting! And there's my *mami* at the pyramid.

Mami! Mami! Look what I found!

Mami says the stone belongs at the Museum of Ancient Art. We can take it there right away. *¡Vámonos!* Let's go!

The museum director says we found an ancient treasure—
the missing piece from the stone jaguar's medallion!

We can put the stone back where it belongs.

We did it! We found and returned the stone. *¡Gracias!* Thanks for helping!